The Key to Christmas

Written by:
Robert Ross

Illustrated by:
Diana McManus Whitman

This book is dedicated to all of those who helped out with the book along the way, as well as my family and all of those wonderful Christmas memories.

The hand inside a wooly red mitten covered in little white fuzzies used a special key to make one final turn of a lock on a door, just beneath a festive wreath.

A deep sigh of relief issued forth as a husky, friendly voice whispered, "Ah! The last one."

As the key was gently removed from the door it began to magically glow as fresh new snowflakes fell upon it from a beautiful moonlit sky.

Standing under the dim porch light, the familiar plump figure with a frosty white beard detached the key from its gold chain that securely held it throughout that night. Then he carefully deposited the shiny instrument into a very tiny coat pocket where it was to be kept safe until next year.

The figure then walked past a window full of Christmas cheer until reaching the porch's edge. He paused for a brief second to pull out a brass gizmo from an unlatched coat pocket and, with those wooly red mittens, he spun it quickly in a clockwise direction.

Within seconds, a Christmas sleigh with it's reindeer encircled the house in a swirly-twirly wind, and swiftly whisked the plump figure away, high up above the rooftops and trees toward the snow-filled sky. If you had been there that night, your ears tilted just right, you would have heard a hefty, friendly voice echoing through the town, exclaiming, "M-E-R-R-Y C-H-R-I-S-T-M-A-S!"

Now, quietly gliding over the landscape as he lifted his arm to wave one last goodbye, a small hole from underneath the jolly man's tiny coat pocket appeared. At a stroke before midnight, the unthinkable happened: unbeknownst to him the Christmas key fell through that hole, bounced off the front seat, and sprung high into the nighttime air as the sleigh disappeared into the distance, leaving the key freefalling behind him.

A howling north wind tossed the key as it fell to earth amidst a smattering of silver Christmas dust that filled the chilly nighttime air.

Within a few moments, the flying object came hurtling through the snowy branches of a large Scotch pine. It was one of many Christmas trees standing ready for sale, leaning up against a fence at the end of a wide-open field.

The Christmas key then sank into a blanket of newly fallen powder.

Santa's most valuable Christmas Eve prize—one that magically glimmered and glowed just a few moments ago—was now like a dying ember among the winter snow that slowly encased it.

The key rested in that spot, unknown and untouched, month after month, season after season until one day, late that next fall …

A stray football tumbled along the leafy open ground, by chance uncovering the key and dislodging it from the broken sticks and cold earth that had covered it for so long.

Toby ran over to pick up his trusty football when he noticed the strange object lying among some leaves and pine needles.

He stuck the football under his arm as he picked up the key and gingerly coddled it in the palm of his hand. "What is this?" Toby mused to himself. "Cool!"

"*Toby, are we gonna play or what?*" yelled an impatient Tiny (who wasn't really tiny but was definitely impatient).

"Hey! What did you find?" someone else yelled.

"Just some change," Toby shouted back as he secretively put the object in his coat pocket and turned back toward the huddle.

The neighborhood game that day was shaping up to be a classic: It was a tie game, and as the football was about to be hiked, both sides stopped and froze for an instant at a collection of somewhat familiar, but distant, noises.

One particular noise sounded like a school bell ringing, but it was muffled by the louder sounds of bustling traffic, shouting voices and loud jack hammers.

I know I have heard those sounds before, Toby thought.

Intrigued, both teams trudged their way through the football field, past the forest of pine trees for sale, so they could get to the damaged part of the fence at the end of the field.

With their fingers clenched onto the broken chain links, the boys peered through the holes in the fence in curiosity at what was happening to their small-valley town below. The football boys scrunched their dirty faces up to the holes, hoping to pinpoint where the sounds were coming from.

"Wow!" they all said, gazing at each other in awe, as a giant hot-air balloon slowly rose over their heads. The logo on the side of it read "The Town of Eagle River's 59th Annual Winter Fun Festival."

"Gosh, that's right! The Winter Fun Festival is almost here!" said Dale.

Vendors and workers of all sorts were doing their best to set up for the extravaganza. Men wearing hard hats hammered stakes into the ground as other workers pumped hot air into colorful balloons. Painters designed welcome signs for visitors arriving at the bus station from out of town.

But the town's noises quickly gave way to the constant clamoring of a bell coming from a house directly across the way. "There's that sound again," Jerry murmured. Everyone turned their heads and focused their attention on Michael's mom standing on her front porch. She was ringing the nightly dinner bell with the same intensity as the conductor of a runaway freight train. Finally, she gave up on the bell and stomped into the house.

"Gotta go, guys," Michael said, and before they knew it, he was on his bike and making his way down the hillside.

"One last play, guys, let's finish the game," Tiny said. Both teams agreed in unison that that was the best course of action at the time.

Before the final snap, Toby wiped the dirt from his old winter vest and blew away the newly fallen snowflakes that covered his worn-out NFL team patch. The rest of the players brushed the debris away from the shiny vinyl sleeves of their brand-new football coats as they lined up for one last battle.

The ball was snapped, and Jeffrey faded back to throw the last pass. Everyone knew it was going to be THE BOMB, including Toby. Most of the players went deep for the pass, but not Toby. He came around the corner and surprised Jeffrey with a hard sack and takedown.

"Game over!" he boasted, but before Toby could celebrate—not even one victory dance—everyone was running down the hill or riding their bikes for home. Toby grabbed his school gear and football. As he made his way to a large gap in the fence that led directly to his house, the curious young lad reached in his pocket and pulled out his newfound treasure.

He stared, admiring it in the fading evening light for a few brief seconds when the headlights from an oncoming car cast a shadow upon one of the neighborhood garages. *Shoot! I gotta get going. Dad will be home soon*, he thought.

He placed the key safely inside his front jean pocket as he tucked the football under his arm. Toby pretended it was the end of a game and he'd have to score a touchdown by reaching the driveway before his father got home or the Bears would lose!

The Bears won.

Toby quickly ran inside his house and he threw his old hand-me-down vest into the front closet. *Why hang it up when I can just throw it in the closet?* he thought, as any typical 12-year-old boy might.

He bolted up the steps as fast as he could, trying to avoid the TV room and the many questions his sister would have for him.

Toby's mind raced as he securely locked the bedroom door behind him.
Let's see … where should I hide this thing?

He carefully scanned the room and decided the best spot would be under his top bunk mattress.

He began climbing the ladder when a new brilliant idea hit him.

Yeah, that's it! No one, especially my sister, would EVER look there. The excited young boy strategically hid it behind his prized army-man collection that was set high on a shelf.

Just then a loud knock came pounding on the bedroom door.

"What are you doing in there, Toby?" Lila asked.

"Nothing! I'll be out in a minute!" Toby reluctantly yelled, still not opening the door.

"Gee! I never get to do anything around here," she said as her feet pitter-pattered down the hallway, a signal that Lila was finally gone.

Toby waited a good 20 seconds for her to go before placing his relic in the secret spot, leaving the room and closing the door behind him.

Toby only made it a few steps down the hallway before he heard a series of loud finger snaps coming from behind him. *Oh, no! My mom! I bet she knows. I'll probably have to hand it over!* Toby thought.

"Toby Ross. Did you wash your hands for dinner?" she asked.
"Uh … no," Toby replied.

He turned his head as instant relief registered on his face.

As the days went by, curiosity got the better of Toby. He wanted to find out more about his discovery, but he was afraid of losing it, so he decided to bring it out only on very special occasions to find out what he could from the people he trusted most.

On Thanksgiving, Toby's family passed it around the dinner table. They took turns as each one of them studied the key's features and speculated as to what it was and where it could have possibly come from.

His dad thought it might have been an old coat pin from the Viking era. His uncle Harold said it was probably an artifact that had belonged to French fur traders who had hunted the area hundreds of years ago. Little cousin Lori was fully convinced it was a key used for starting alien spaceships.

Every Sunday afternoon, Toby's grandpa Aki stopped at the house for dinner after attending church. On this day, Toby showed him the mysterious key. Grandpa Aki carefully held the object up to the dining room light and examined its unique shape and the artistry of its work. The family highly valued his opinion, since he was a family expert in the field of archaeology. He said it was possibly some sort of religious cross from an ancient South American culture.

Everyone seemed to have a different opinion! With no concrete answers, Toby decided the best course of action would be to take it to class for show and tell and have his classmates give their opinions, too. Plus, his teacher, Mrs. Griffith, seemed to know a lot about history and geography so he thought maybe she could shed some light upon its origin.

The next day, Mrs. Griffith had her turn at the mysterious key. She sat at her desk, truly mesmerized by the object in her hands. After studying it for a long time, she finally concluded that it was more than likely a piece of Native American jewelry from the Great Plains, made sometime in the 1400s.

At the end of the school day during show and tell, Toby described how he found the object and his classmates took turns passing it around, speculating as to what it was. At one point, the room had grown too warm and stuffy with all the commotion. Mrs. Griffith gave Toby permission to open one of the classroom windows to let some cool winter air in. Just as he opened the window, a powerful gust of winter wind blew into the classroom, sending powdery snowflakes throughout the room—and onto the key now back in Toby's hand. At the very moment when the snow hit the key, something strange and wonderful happened, to the amazement of everyone watching—the thing lit up like a moonbeam! Its glow was unearthly, magical.

It was glowing so bright that the class turned off the lights to better see it beam. It was like nothing they had ever seen before. Toby couldn't believe what he held in his hands. After that episode, everyone seemed to want it for themselves, so Toby buried the valuable piece deep in his pocket.

Weeks later, as Christmas break loomed, Toby squirmed in his seat at his school desk. He tried hard to listen to the teacher but his attention was squarely focused on the clock.

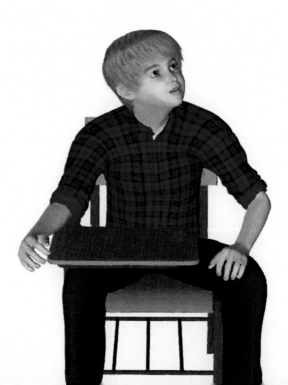

With the holiday season quickly approaching, and this being the last day of school before winter break, it would be next to impossible for him to concentrate on his studies.

Mrs. Griffith sat on the edge of her desk, instructing the class about fire safety. "Make sure to water the tree every day during Christmas break, kids."
Amid a bounty of gift baskets, small wrapped presents, chocolates, and various other holiday gifts from her students, she continued with her speech.

"I'm sorry, I must be rambling on," she said. "I just want you all to have a very Merry Christmas and …

"Come on, come on, ring!" Toby said to himself.

At that point, the whole class was staring rather intently at the clock. They hadn't heard a thing that Mrs. Griffith had said for the past 10 minutes or so. Just then, the Franklin School bell rang and everyone ran for the door, grabbing their coats and a month's worth of art projects.

"Be careful, and happy holidays everyone!" Mrs. Griffith hollered at the class as they crashed into her.

The hallways quickly jammed full of yelling and screaming students who were just let out of school jail for the holiday season. Hordes of jubilant kids made their way out onto the sidewalks and into their designated school buses.

While riding bus number 7, Toby and his sister sat by each other singing Christmas songs with the other riders. The last day of school before winter break was always a very special ride home. Every kid on the bus was allowed to sing Christmas carols at the tops of their lungs.

The bus rumbled through various neighborhoods dropping off kids who were full of holiday cheer. As the bus turned the corner and made its way down Jay Street, everyone started bouncing on their bus seat in anticipation of "the bump."

"The bump" was just that—a huge bump that ran all the way across the road. All the kids knew about "the bump" but rarely attempted to bounce in their seats out of utter fear that Mrs. Barker, the bus driver, might eat them alive. Mrs. Barker only took her focus off the bus's giant rear view mirror on two special occasions: The last day of school and the day before Christmas break.

Just before the bus hit its mark, everyone began bouncing. As the bus roared over "the bump," the whole school bus erupted in laughter, including Mrs. Barker, as a number of kids' stocking hats nearly touched the top of the bus.

Toby and Lila laughed and smiled as they wrestled their way through the front door of the house.

"Mom! Mom!" the two of them bellowed.

"Where is she?" they said to each other.

"I'm in here," Mrs. Ross called out.

Usually their mom was in the kitchen when the kids got home, either preparing a snack or making dinner, but that day she was planted in the living room.

"What are you doing in here?" the two of them asked.

Mrs. Ross had a certain gleam in her eye. She stood in the living room directly in front of the picture window near the family Christmas tree, holding her hands behind her back.

"Close your eyes," she said. As both kids closed their eyes, Mrs. Ross slowly brought out the surprise from behind her back.

The two excited kids glanced over at one another, then raced as fast as they could to snatch the special Winter Christmas catalog from her hands.

The next best thing to getting actual presents on Christmas was being able to pick out the toys you wanted from Santa in the Winter Christmas catalog.

They both tore through the pages in record time as they sat in front of the Christmas tree, eating the candy from their advent calendars.

Mom reached over the couch and handed each of them a blank piece of paper and a pencil. Lila's toy section came first as she began to write down her Christmas list. "I want that and that ... oh, and that!" she yelled as she flipped through the catalog pages.

When it was Toby's turn, he grabbed the catalog and furiously wrote down item after item with page numbers for each one. *There's no way Santa could mistake what I want if I write down the page numbers, he thought. This is truly a genius system.*

"Well! Anyone home?" said Mr. Ross, as he shoved open the front door and brushed away the newly fallen snow from his hat.

Lila ran over to her dad. He picked her up and set her high upon his shoulder. An overwhelming smile beamed across Toby's face as he hugged his father and gave him a high five.

Toby's father set his hat down and he hurriedly made his way to the basement. When he reentered the living room, he was carrying several boxes plainly marked with the word "CHRISTMAS."

"Well?! Are you two going to help me or what?" Mr. Ross asked. Toby's eyes lit up as he and Lila peeled through box after box of the family's holiday ornaments, many of them handed down from generations past.

The smell of doughy sugar cookies wafted through the festive air as the family spent the rest of the night decorating the Christmas tree and listening to Christmas music.

The next night, Toby jubilantly jumped down the stairs, making his way toward the kitchen for dinner when he happened to notice some noise coming from the TV room. "Why are we eating in the … ?"

He almost forgot that it was the biggest TV night of the year—the Christmas specials were on!

Toby's mom had strategically placed the kid's TV trays directly in front of the huge 19-inch Zenith TV for optimal viewing pleasure. Both kids looked at each other and grinned from ear to ear. Nothing quite signaled the beginning of the Christmas season like the Christmas shows. Lila and Toby enthusiastically ate their frozen dinners while watching the best Christmas programs of the season.

It seemed official now; the Christmas holiday was in full swing and it wouldn't be long before the big day arrived. Oh! Pure joy and excitement had fully set in. The two of them always so looked forward to the upcoming holiday festivities.

That night, both kids had settled into their cozy spots on the couch, thoroughly enjoying show after show until Toby realized something while watching *The Grinch Who Stole Christmas* that changed his whole demeanor. He slowly put down his fish stick when it occurred to him that the shows depicted Santa entering each and every house by going DOWN THE CHIMNEY.

Wait a minute—how could the Grinch, or Santa, or anyone for that matter, deliver presents by using the chimney? "I never really noticed that before," Toby said to himself. *How could I have missed such a simple detail like that?*

Poor Toby put his tray aside as he sank back into the couch.

He tried his best to pretend to enjoy the festive shows for his sister's sake, but his reflection in the TV said it all: a blank stare was all he could muster on his face. The fact of the matter is, once you know something, you can't un-know it.

Late that night, while Toby lay still in his bed, it seemed that all his holiday joy had been crushed deep within him as he thought about what he may have uncovered.

Come down the chimney? It just isn't possible, he thought.

As he stared at the ceiling, a small teardrop of holiday spirit leaked out, streaming down his red, rosy cheek and onto his pillow.

When Toby awoke the next morning, he was deep beneath a thick layer of covers. And still sad.

"Toby, hurry up!" his mom yelled from the downstairs kitchen. "Your dad's got the car running!"

Toby casually put on his clothes and moped down the hallway where he continued his slow descent down the stairs that seemed much longer that morning.

"Mom, where are we going?" Toby reluctantly asked.

"To the sledding hill, remember?" she replied.

Mr. Ross honked the horn from the garage.

Toby's mother opened the side door to the kitchen to grab Toby's snow boots. Toby caught a glimpse of the car running with the garage door wide open. Sitting all bundled up behind the wheel and ready to go was Toby's dad. Lila was on the front arm rest waving furiously for Toby to come.

Wait a minute. Maybe I could get some answers at the *sledding hill*, he thought. *I know my cousins will all be there, and my cousin Mark knows everything!*

Toby gazed out the car window as he took mental notes on just how many houses *didn't* have chimneys. He shook his head in dismay.

"What's the matter, son?" asked Mr. Ross as he looked at Toby from his rearview mirror. Toby started to tell his dad about his predicament, but then he stopped himself. He just couldn't get up the courage.

"We're here!" shouted Lila.

Mr. Ross parked the old wagon in a nearby abandoned parking lot where he opened the back hatch to pull out the kids' favorite sleds.

Lila paced back and forth in excitement as her dad reached in and gave her the "Red Beauty." It was a plastic sled, a disc really, upon which she had placed a bunch of stickers. She had gotten it the previous year for Christmas.

Then he grabbed Toby's classic sled: the Radio Flyer. It was a real rocket—a one-man toboggan with a wooden deck outlined in deep red with white trim. The words RADIO FLYER were hand-painted on the front near the steering column. Oh, how Toby loved that old sled!

After walking for what seemed like 10 miles next to a busy two-lane road, the three of them finally reached the sledding hill where their cousins were waiting for them.

"I thought you'd never get here," Mark smirked. "I estimate there must be roughly 65 people on the hill today."

"Boy! That Mark sure is smart," Toby murmured to his sister. Then, the whole bunch jumped on their sleds and flew down the hill.

Everyone was having a fabulous time going up and down the sledding hill late into the day when Mark approached both Toby and Lila. He proudly stood next to them, holding his primo orange plastic sled, and stated, "I'm going down the jump hill. I figure that if I hit the jump at 24 miles an hour, I should easily break the record."

There was a long pause.

"Well, is anyone else coming, or what?!" Mark asked.

Both Toby and Lila shook their heads

"Oh, come on!" Mark insisted.

"No way!" Toby said rather sternly, "And Lila's still too small, anyway."

Lila nodded her head in agreement with the rest of the relatives who looked to be in complete shock.

Very few brave souls ever even attempted the outrageous daredevil stunt, let alone on such a cold and icy day.

Now was the time to ask Mark, Toby thought, before he kills himself.
"Hey, Mark! How do you think Santa goes down all those chimneys?"

Mark shrugged his shoulders and said, "How do I know? I've never really thought about it. Maybe Santa goes on a diet before Christmas."

Toby stood there like an ice sculpture, partly in awe of Mark's answer, and partly for his willingness to tackle the most dangerous hill on the planet.

Before anyone could try and talk him out of it, Mark's adrenaline kicked in, and he took off!

His sled looked as if it was going 65 miles an hour when it hit the ramp, almost sideways. The image of Mark kicking his arms and legs in midair is still discussed reverently by Highland sledders to this day.

Mark screamed in sheer terror as he flew off the sled and landed directly into the path of oncoming sled traffic. It was an ugly scene as sled after sled ran into and over him.

The two dads raced to the bottom of the hill. After a few anxious moments, Toby and the rest of the onlookers clapped as Mark got back on his feet with help from his dad, who carried Mark like a wounded soldier.

Lila and Toby had already started to make their way to the car when Mr. Ross pointed to the parking lot and picked up the twisted remains of Mark's orange sled.

The day of sledding on the hill was over.

Toby wet his hair and hand brushed it while looking in the mirror.

"Let's go. We don't want to be late tonight!" his dad yelled from the bottom step.

Waiting patiently, with the front door wide open, were Lila, Mrs. Ross, and Toby's aunt Janny, who was visiting from San Diego.

The ladies simply couldn't wait any longer so they made their way to the station wagon.

"I'm coming," Toby grudgingly replied, as he took one more long look at himself in the mirror.

"This is going to be the worst Christmas ever. I just know it," he said to himself as he sluggishly made his way to the bottom of the stairs.

"Everything alright, sport?" his dad asked. "Come on, it's almost Christmas. You should be happy!" his dad said as he put his arm around Toby and shut the door.

It was just a two days before Christmas, and the Ross family was on their way to make their annual round of Christmas activities. Their first stop was a large rented hall to meet their families that included some small Italian ladies who kept everyone's plates filled with food while the kids played board games throughout the night.

After that, it was on to St. Mary's Church for a late-night Christmas service, where everyone but Toby sang page after page of holiday hymns. The children's group then acted out the birth of Jesus on the stage.

Finally, the night ended at their aunt's house, where family members gathered to eat Swedish meatballs and drink orange punch.

Usually, these holiday festivities flew by for Toby, but this year, it seemed as if it was the longest Christmas season of all time. He just couldn't get his mind off Santa's dilemma.

On the way home, Toby's glum young face peered out the cold, frosty station wagon window at all the houses that were overly decorated for the holidays.

One house had a glowing plastic Santa on the roof, entering the house through its chimney. It was just too much. That's when Toby closed his eyes for the night.

With two kids slumped over his shoulders, Mr. Ross carefully placed them both in their beds, one by one, being careful not to wake them. It had been a long night of Christmas festivities.

Toby was fast asleep when he was awakened by the sound of shuffling feet on the snowy front porch.

Moments later came a soft knock on the door. Toby heard the faint voice of his aunt Janny talking to a man downstairs.

Fascinated by the conversation, he lay motionless trying to hear the discussion, but the distant voices were too muffled to make out what they were saying, so he quietly got down from his top bunk and pressed himself against the spindles of the upstairs handrail.

"I'm sorry to bother you, especially so close to Christmas," the tiny man said to Toby's aunt Janny. "Last year I was in town on some business about this time when I seemed to have lost a very important key. You don't know of anyone who may have found an old key, now do you?"

Toby quickly perked up.

"No … no, I can't say that I do, but I'm from out of town. Was this a bank key or something?" said Aunt Janny.

"Oh, no. It's a magnificent key," the man said as a curious Toby peeked his head just above the railing to get a better look.

"The key is worth far more than money. It's a key that brings hope and joy to many people."

He continued to explain more about the key, right down to its shape and size and how it changes in appearance only on Christmas Eve. He even talked about how it glowed when snow fell upon it.

"You can see its beautiful, bright light when snow hits it. And from where I live, it lights up the whole night sky!" he said.

"I'm afraid that if I don't get that key back very soon …" He paused and lowered his head.

"Sounds like whoever found a key like that would be lucky," Aunt Janny said as she offered him some hot cocoa that he most gratefully guzzled down in record time.

"You're quite right," the man said as he handed her the empty mug.

Then he picked up his small satchel and handed Janny his business card as she escorted him to the door.

He told her to give him a jingle, which Toby found a little curious, if she came across any information pertaining to the key.

"Sorry about your key. I do hope you find it. And Merry Christmas!" Aunt Janny said as she closed the door behind the kind stranger.

Toby snuck back to his room trying hard not to think about what had just happened.

While sitting on the edge of his bed, he thought for a long time that night about the conflict going on inside his head.

"It's my key. I'm the one who found it," Toby said quietly to himself.

He tried desperately to go to sleep and forget what the man had said. He tossed and turned, clutching the key in his hand.

What should I do? What should I do?!

Finally, he couldn't take it anymore and decided to do something.

First, Toby put the key around his neck for safe keeping. Then Toby went to the closet where he loaded a football, some warm clothes, and several valuable items from his dresser drawer into a small duffle bag. On his bed, he shattered his piggy bank and grabbed a handful of money—close to 30 dollars. Very quietly and slowly, he snuck down the stairs and took his NFL vest from the front closet.

As he carefully tiptoed over the phone cord that stretched from the TV room to the kitchen, a glimmer of light from the nearby room cast a shadow on the kitchen table. Toby had looked over the mysterious mans business card very carefully before shoving it into his duffle bag.

Before attempting to open the back door, Toby made sure to be very careful because that particular door made an annoying squeaky sound if you did it too quickly. The young boy carefully twisted the door knob just the right way before popping it quietly open and escaping into the dark, snowy night.

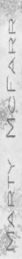

11114 Toy Street,

MARTY McFARR

NORTH POLE

1 - NorthPole

Toby sprinted down the street to the football field, through the hole in the fence and past the Christmas trees that were for sale. He decided to pause for a moment to collect his thoughts.

He reached into his duffle bag and retrieved the old business card.

"Marty McFarr, 1-1-1-1-4 …?"

The rest of it was too hard to read, so he moved the card around, trying to find bright enough moonlight that would allow him to read the small print.

"1-1-1-1-4 Toy Street, North Pole."

"North Pole!" he exclaimed to himself.

His heart began to pound so hard in his chest he thought he might pass out. Reaching into his pocket, he felt for the key. Still there! But as he pulled it out, the cold hard object slipped between his fingers and fell to the ground. *I can't afford to lose this.* Thinking fast, Toby picked up the key and tore off a piece of his vest, threaded it through the top of the key, and then placed it around his neck for safekeeping.

From his spot high on the hill, Toby thoroughly scanned the bus station down below, but could see no buses going in or out. The station was closed.

North Pole? he thought. "How am I going to get there now?"

Just then, a steamy, warm gush of air from an ascending hot air balloon blew the boy back onto the frozen ground.

Eagle Rivers
59th Annual
Winter Fun
Festival

Toby jumped to his feet, brushed himself off and tried to clear the cobwebs. He gazed down into the valley below where he spotted a bright red hot air balloon shooting up the narrow ridge rather quickly in front of him.

Inside the balloon's basket there seemed to be a lone small figure waving wildly… at him?

Amazingly, it was Lila!

"Get in!" she yelled. "Hurry! I'm scared!"

Several workers below were in a frenzy.

Toby took a few steps backwards, threw his duffle bag over his right shoulder, and climbed carefully out onto the narrow ridge.

The brave young soul waited just a few seconds for the exact moment when the balloon would be within striking distance before making the giant leap. He then pushed off the ridge with all his might, unfortunately his foot slipped off the icy edge and he lost his traction. Missing his mark, his hands slammed into the side of the basket—not what he had planned! Toby hung on for dear life, his heart now pounding so violently in his chest he thought that might end up killing him. Lila rushed over to try and help him, but his grip quickly gave way and he found himself suddenly free falling. *This can't be happening!*

As he fell, at the very last moment, Toby reached out and grasped one of the dangling ropes. It caught him up sharply but kept him alive! He took a second to catch his breath, then shimmied his way up the rope and into the basket to safety.

"What are you doing here?" he asked Lila.

"I thought you might need some help," she explained with a big smile on her face. Despite almost plummeting to his certain death, he was happy to see her.

"Lila, it's a key! Do you believe it?" Toby asked.

"I know. I was hiding behind the couch, spying on Christmas presents when the little man came in."

The two of them hugged, then looked at each other in amazement as they floated above their little town.

"It's our duty to get this key back to its rightful owner, don't you think?" Toby asked.

Lila agreed.

The balloon continued to climb high into the sky as the two of them glanced back to take one last look before embarking on their adventure.

Within a few minutes, the little town of Eagle River quickly disappeared from sight. Slowly and steadily, their hot-air fortress made its way northward.

Toby constantly checked his compass throughout the night to make sure they were on course and headed directly for the North Pole. At times, they both peeked over the edge of the basket in awe as they made their way over numerous small towns and dense snow covered forests.

A set of fading city lights in the distance was their last view of civilization. Only a flicker from the balloon's fire cast a faint illumination out onto miles and miles of the upcoming cold, barren landscape.

Miles and miles now separated the kids from their home. Toby and Lila's adventure took them over the tops of white snow-peaked mountains and across what seemed to be a thousand lakes. Toby reached over the edge of the basket to pull up a loose rope when he spotted a lone wolf howling at the eerie Northern Lights.

Every minute that went by, Toby could feel they were making their way closer and closer to their destination.

"We're almost there, aren't we, Toby?" Lila asked.

Toby grabbed her hand to help reassure her when he sensed a rapid change in the weather. The two young travelers looked up and spotted a mass of dark clouds looming ahead. In fear, Lila tightly gripped Toby's hand as a fierce winter squall quickly approached. The children quickly braced themselves for the blizzard to hit.

The fierce winter storm was too big, and it came too fast for them to try and go around it. The balloon wouldn't be able to dodge a storm that size anyway. Their only chance was to ride it out.

"Grab a rope, tie it around your waist and hang on!" Toby shouted through the roaring gusts of wind that suddenly engulfed them.

In desperation, Toby pulled the heat cord to try and get the balloon to rise above the thunder and snow, but the cord snapped, sending the two of them stumbling to the opposite side of the basket.

Lila screamed as the rushing wind blew the basket from side to side. One of the basket's ropes broke free from the balloon, causing it to tilt sideways. They were on the brink of falling out when Toby reached in his shirt for the key—but it was gone!

He crawled over to Lila as snow and debris whipped wildly overhead. The two of them huddled together in the corner holding onto each other, feeling more scared than ever.

"We're sinking fast!" she yelled as they began to rapidly lose altitude. "And we're headed right for that glacier!"

Toby grabbed her with all his might and threw her to the other side of the basket. The brave boy then dove next to her and attempted to cover her as the tattered remains of the balloon came crashing to the ground.

Did we just crash-land a hot air balloon!? Toby looked down at his sister—yes, they had just survived something unbelievable! The two hugged each other, grateful to be alive. Just then, a seabird flew in and landed on the rim of their basket. Toby knew from his studies in school that this was a species that lived in the Arctic Circle, called the guillemot—pronounced GILL-A-MOTT. His teacher, Mrs. Muller, had made them say it out loud.

The bird's piercing eyes looked directly at them, and it made a loud screeching sound as if it were mocking the two adventurers.

They sat and watched with curiosity as it flew down and started nibbling on some graham cracker crumbs that were scattered on the basket's floor.

Suddenly the winged creature decided to use its webbed feet to grab something that was hidden underneath the duffle bag. What was it?

The guillemot spread its wings and readjusted itself and began to fly off. "Oh no! The key!" Toby cried out.

Thinking quickly, he reached inside his nearby duffle bag and pulled out his weapon of choice—a football. With a tight grip, Toby threw a perfect spiral, striking the bird in the head.

Bingo!

The flying thief hit the side of the gondola, dropping the key from its claws before screeching one last time and flying off into the dark night.

The key string now clung precariously to the side of the broken basket as it fluttered in the frigid wind, threatening to blow away at any moment. Lila ran to grab the string but she slipped and fell.

Toby hurried over to her, reaching desperately for the key string just as a polar blast of Arctic air threw the basket sideways. The children toppled over with it, unable to regain their footing.

The basket hurtled and skidded along the frosty ground before slamming into the side of the glacier, breaking the basket nearly in half and launching the key out onto the open tundra.

The battered basket spun around and fell into a huge crevice at the edge of the glacier, but not before the deflated balloon itself came to an abrupt halt when it became ensnared on a jagged piece of ice sending the kids tumbling outside the basket.

With the basket teetering on the brink of the iceberg, both kids hung onto some dangling ropes as Toby yelled into the howling wind, "Lila, get on my back! We'll piggyback our way up, and don't look down!"

As they climbed the perilous ropes, winter's blast slammed them brutally into the icy mountain glacier, time and time again. At one point, the duffle bag hit the frozen wall and fell from Toby's shoulder, sending it hurtling into the depths of the crevice. But Toby didn't have time to mourn his loss. He had to focus on his task.

"Almost there, Lila!" Toby tried hard to reassure her. Just then, one of the remaining ropes above them snapped from the balloon. That's when Toby realized they were still attached to the basket. Not good. *If the basket goes down, then we go down.*

With one hand, he quickly unraveled Lila's rope. He then untied the rope from around his own waist right before it completely broke free of the balloon smashed into the icy rocks below.

"Almost to the top now, Lila. I can see the balloon!" he said. "Hang on. You're doing great!" She silently clung to her big brother, trying her best not to be heavy.

Toby reached out to grasp the top of the balloon when the whole thing tore free from the icy ridge and started to give way. Toby kept grabbing and grasping onto the balloon as the slick material slid between his fingers. If he could only reach something solid up top, they would be okay.

Lila let out a loud scream as she began to slide off of Toby's back. "Toby!" she shrieked as she began to fall. That's when Toby did what big brothers do in situations like this—reacting with split-second timing, he grabbed onto the hood of Lila's coat with one hand while continuing to hang onto the end of the balloon with his other hand.

Now as he desperately held on to Lila and about to lose his grip, the balloon suddenly caught onto something and stopped falling.

It was Santa's sleigh! Fortunately, the rails touched down just in time to catch the very tip of the balloon, holding it in place.

Toby managed to use the rest of the deflated balloon to pull Lila and himself up over the ridge to safety. Exhausted and out of breath, the two of them lay on the ground next to the great sleigh for what seemed a very long time.

After resting atop the ice, they became aware of their surroundings and were amazed at the glowing winter scene around them. "Toby, look!" yelled Lila as the clouds and snow lifted.

"Cool!" said Toby as he gazed upon an icy snow village sparkling in the far-off distance.

"I'm happy to see that you two are okay," Santa said as he stood behind them, holding the infamous key in his red wooly mitten with the little white fuzzies on it.

"I don't know what I'd have done without my key!" Santa explained. "I want to thank you two for coming all this way to return it. Now, what are your names?"

"My name is Toby, sir, and that's my sister Lila."

Both youngsters turned and smiled at each other.

"We have taken good care of it, Santa, sir," Lila tried to explain.

The snow crunched under Santa's feet as he made his way over to his Christmas sleigh.

"Very good! I think I lost it about this time last year," said Santa in a relieved and jovial voice.

"I was the one who really found the key, Santa. We were trying desperately to get it to you in time for Christmas," said Toby.

"Yes, I see. Well! Toby and Lila, what you two were attempting to do was very brave and courageous," Santa said. "And it's just in time! I was about to make my Christmas Eve run and it would have been nearly impossible to spread all that Christmas joy without my key! I might have had to try and go down chimneys if it weren't for you two," said Santa as he chuckled, lodging himself in the driver's seat.

He then grabbed the sleigh's reins tightly, "Well, are you two coming?" he said in a spirited voice.

"Back home?" Toby asked.

"Ho, ho, ho … No!" Santa said. "We have a lot of Christmas cheer to deliver before that!"

Flabbergasted, the two jolly kids jumped into Santa's sleigh.

Santa winked at the two of them and snickered as he reached into one of his coat pockets. He then pulled out his brass gizmo and spun the top of it as his sleigh and reindeer, full of Christmas toys, swooped down into a fog of swirling air. The great sleigh then disappeared into the frosty, dark night.

Within seconds, Santa and his new helpers were standing under a bright moon in front of a beautiful wooden door. Lila and Toby stood there like two ice sculptures with presents in hand, not knowing what to do.

"Here. Try this, son," Santa said.

He reached over Toby's shoulder and stuck out his big red mitten. Dangling in front of the boy on a gold key chain was Toby's string with Santa's Christmas key still fastened to it.

Santa unlatched the key and said, "Go ahead. You've earned it!"

Toby set his presents down into the crackling snow. His hand trembled in excitement as he inserted the Christmas key into the lock.

CLICK! The heavy front door came slightly ajar.

"That's incredible," Toby said.

All three of them tiptoed quietly into the house and placed all the presents under the tree. Santa then ate all the Christmas cookies that were left for him on the kitchen table. Not even a crumb was left behind.

As the magical night went on, Santa's Christmas sleigh streaked across the sky, moving from house to house with incredible speed. At every new door, Santa and the kids opened each one with his trusty ol' Christmas key.

Before Toby and Lila knew it, the tub of presents was nearly empty, and the sleigh came to a stop in front of their house.

"What?! We're back home already? This is the last one, isn't it?" a disappointed Toby asked Santa.

"I'm making this house my special, final stop this year," said Santa.

Lila and her brother climbed out and reluctantly walked to their front door.

Toby made a slow turn toward Santa as he took off his red wooly mitten and extended his hand.

"Thank you, sir," Toby said.

"No. Thank you!" said Santa as he shook Toby's hand. "You better get inside now."

"Okay, if we have to," Lila said to Santa as she gave him a big hug. "Good night, Santa."

"Good night, Lila," the jolly man said, hugging her back. "You kids better get upstairs and into bed. You don't want to be on the naughty list now, do you?"

"No! And thank you for getting us home, Santa," Toby said as he shook Santa's mitten once again.

He then put his arm around his little sister, and they both quietly walked inside the house, closing the door behind them but not before taking one more look at Santa.

Toby climbed into bed that night replaying the incredible adventure over and over in his mind. It was almost too good to believe. *Did that really just happen?*

Pure joy set in as he thought about he and Lila opening door after door as they tiptoed through each house with excitement and wonder. He thought about Lila grabbing presents and placing them under people's sparkling Christmas trees, and the Christmas sleigh zooming across the night sky.

As the young boy began to drift off to sleep, a single tear rolled down his cheek, rolling off his face and falling softly onto the pillow. But this wasn't a tear of sadness or disappointment—this time it was a tear of Christmas joy.

Outside the house at 743 Harvey Street, his job complete, Santa's red mitten turned the key one last time that night. It was then—with great care—that the key was secured in Santa's mended pocket, thanks to Mrs. Claus and her handy sewing skills.

He made one quick tug on the pocket to be sure it was good and safe before getting into his sleigh where he was swept off the front porch by a swirly-twirly wind, vanishing into the night.

Toby woke up that Christmas morning with a feeling of happiness in his heart.

He climbed down the ladder of the top bunk in a frenzy. Lila was already awake. She grabbed his shirt and began shouting, "Christmas is here! Christmas is here!"

Both youngsters sprinted into their parents' room, creating a cyclone of glee and childlike joy.

Toby and Lila flew down the stairs, dragging their parents behind them as they burst into the living room, as every child who loves Christmas does on this day each year.

The joyful frenzy began. In record time all the presents had been opened, and the joy of gift giving didn't stop until colorful shreds of wrapping paper covered the entire living room floor.

Later that day, in front of the picture window, Toby's fingers flew over the keys of his new handheld electronic football game when Michael came running by the house with what looked to be a new football in his hands.

Stopping on the sidewalk in front of their house, he motioned for Toby to come outside.

"Mom, can I go out and play football?" Toby asked.

"Yes! But only for a little while. We're going to your uncle's for Christmas dinner," she replied.

Toby ran over to the closet to throw on his old vest.

He had trouble finding it as he brushed aside coats and hangers. He was about to call for his mom when he noticed a hanger somewhat hidden at the back of the closet in a shiny, thick wrap of plastic.

"Wow!" exclaimed Toby. His eyes lit up like a Christmas tree.

It was a brand-new football jacket just like his friends had with his favorite team's logo on it!

"It's even got the matching hat, too!" he said to himself with glee

Toby ran excitedly out of the house and down the sidewalk. When he reached the familiar hole in the fence, he put his hands in his new coat's pockets to try and warm them up. And there he discovered a wonderful surprise: It was the key string from his old vest!

He took the string out and tied it, one last time, around his neck, where it would stay forever to remind him of that special, magical Christmas

Toby's feet were 10 feet off the ground when he played the football game that day. Never before had he felt so happy and full of Christmas joy. He made some spectacular one-handed, diving catches, and threw several long touchdown passes that amazed his friends.

At one point, Toby stood in the middle of the field, admiring the Christmas colors that surrounded him. He felt the crisp, vinyl sleeves of his new coat as he wiped away the fresh, new powder that began to fall upon it.

In that moment, Toby realized something amazing: he had gotten his Christmas spirit back. From then on … he never lost it.